The Hungry Thing Goes to a Restaurant

by JAN SLEPIAN and ANN SEIDLER

Pictures by ELROY FREEM

Scholastic Inc.

New York   Toronto   London   Auckland   Sydney

For my newest Things, Micah and Brian
J.S.

And for mine, William, Nicholas, Daniel, and Tess
A.S.

ISBN 0-590-45525-7

12 11 9 8 7 6 5 4 3 2 1   4 5 6 7/9

Printed in the U.S.A.   09

First Scholastic printing, December 1992

One day, the Hungry Thing went to a restaurant. He carried a big sack.

A boy named Buster sat on the steps with his twin sister Sue. Buster said, "Hi, Hungry Thing."

The Hungry Thing pointed to a sign around his neck. It said **FEED ME.**

Sue said, "We're hungry, too."

The Hungry Thing took them into the restaurant.

The headwaiter looked down his nose and said, "We don't serve Things here. Not even Hungry ones."

The Hungry Thing
ate some napkins.

The headwaiter changed
his mind. "Sit right
down, sir."

But he said no to the
twins. "Shoo. Go away.
No children allowed."

The Hungry Thing sat down on his sack.
He hid the twins behind his back. He pointed
to the sign around his neck. It said **FEED ME.**

The headwaiter said, "Would you like a drink?"

The Hungry Thing nodded. "Bapple moose,"
he said.

The headwaiter said to the waitress, "Bapple moose? What's that? Oh, my! Quick, tell me, or he'll eat my tie."

"Let me see," said the waitress. "I think it's a tea. It's for soaking your feet while up in a tree."

"I disagree," said the waiter.
"It is boiled in a pail. You pour it
on seaweed when serving
a whale."

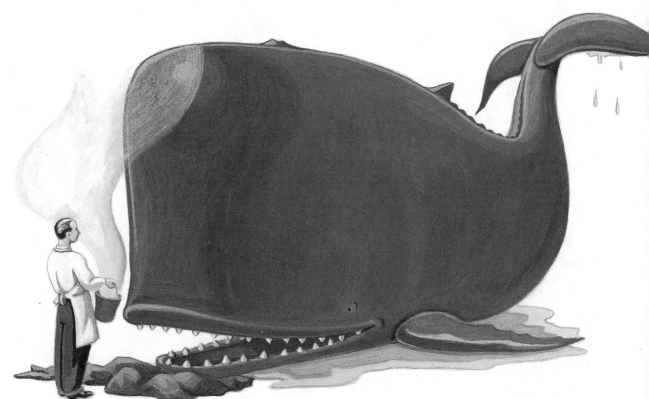

Buster and his sister Sue laughed.
The headwaiter found them.
   The twins said, "Bapple moose sounds like . . .
sapple goose. Sounds like . . . APPLE JUICE to us."

"Of course," said the waitress. She rolled in a barrel of apple juice for the Hungry Thing. He drank it all up.

The headwaiter shook his head at the twins. "Shoo. Go away. No children allowed."

The Hungry Thing hid the twins under the table. He pointed to his sign that said **FEED ME.**

"What would you like to eat?" asked the headwaiter.

"Spoonadish," said the Hungry Thing.

The headwaiter said to the waitress, "Spoonadish? Do we have it, by chance? Quick, tell me, or he'll eat my pants."

"I've heard tell,"
said the waitress.
"It comes in a shell.
It is served to large frogs
when they're not feeling well."

"I disagree," said the waiter.
"It's really a cake, made of mustard
and fleas, as a treat for a snake."

Buster and his sister
Sue laughed. The
headwaiter found them
under the table.
The twins said,
"Spoonadish sounds like
... loonafish. Sounds like
... TUNA FISH to us."

"Of course!" said the waiter. He set a tub
of tuna fish before the Hungry Thing.
The Hungry Thing ate it all up.

   The headwaiter shook his finger at the twins.
"Shoo. Go away. No children allowed."

The Hungry Thing hid
the twins under his tail.
He pointed to his sign
that said **FEED ME.**
The headwaiter said,
"You have had your fill.
It is time to pay the bill."

The Hungry Thing ate the tablecloth.
The headwaiter said, "Yessir, I see what
you mean, sir. What would you like to eat, sir?"
"Bench flies," said the Hungry Thing.

The headwaiter said to the waitress, "Bench flies! Is that something new? Quick, tell me, or he'll eat my shoe."

"It is said," claimed the waitress, "they are bones wrapped in bread. They are eaten by tigers while reading in bed."

"I agree," said the waiter. "And when stirred into stews, make a popular toothpaste for girl kangaroos."

Buster and his sister Sue laughed. The headwaiter found them again.

The twins said, "Bench flies sounds like . . . mench pies. Sounds like . . . FRENCH FRIES to us."

"Of course!" said the waiter. He wheeled out a cart full of French fries.

The Hungry Thing didn't touch a one. "Smetchup," he added.

The headwaiter threw his hands in the air. "Oh, dear, oh, dear, is smetchup on the menu here?"

"It is not," said the waitress. "Smetchup's too hot. Smoke comes out of your ears if you're eating a lot."

"I disagree,"
said the waiter.
"Smetchup's a pie.
It makes you fly,
but I don't know why!"

Buster and Sue both cried,
"Ketchup! The Hungry Thing
wants his French fries
with ketchup!"

"Are you *still* here? Shoo!
Go away. No children allowed,"
said the headwaiter.

"They're okay. Let them stay,"
said a lady dressed in gray.

"Yes, please do, we want you to,"
said her sister dressed in blue.

"Hey, there, Mac, what's in the sack?"
asked a man dressed in black.

The Hungry Thing
pointed to his sign
that said **FEED ME.**
"Hopsicles," he requested.
The twins took charge.
"He wants Popsicles,"
they said.

"Silk snakes," said
the Hungry Thing.

"Milk shakes,"
ordered the twins.

"Born on the slob,"
said the Hungry Thing.

"Corn on the cob!"
shouted the twins.

The waiters brought out trays of food piled high with Popsicles, milk shakes, and corn on the cob. Everyone in the restaurant gathered around to watch.

The headwaiter waved the bill.

"You don't pay! You don't stay!
All three of you must go away."

The Hungry Thing wiped his mouth on the headwaiter's tie. He sat Buster and his sister Sue at the table. Then he opened his sack.
Out poured a pile of money.

He turned his sign around.
It said **FEED THEM.**
Everyone in the restaurant cheered.

The Hungry Thing smiled and bowed.
He patted his stomach and went away.